Zac's Mighty Wheels and the Giant Problem

By Andrea Kurth and Owen Kurth

Illustrated by Emily Gudzinski

Greenhouse Press

This book is a work of fiction. Names, characters, places, and incidents are either products of the author's imagination or are used fictitiously.

Library of Congress Number: 2021906200

Printed in the United States of America

First printing April 2021

Paperback ISBN: 978-1-7369403-0-3
Hardcover ISBN: 978-1-7369403-1-0
eBook ISBN: 978-1-7369403-2-7

Edited by Nadara "Nay" Merrill
www.thatgrammargal.com
and Sarah Wynne
www.littlebirdediting.co.uk
Book design by DTPerfect.com

www.kurthbooks.com

For Zachary Davis, a true superhero in life,
who inspired me and everyone he knew.
AK

For all teachers and the knowledge
they give to our kids.
EG

Contents

Chapter 1

The Wishing Well

"I spy something green," Zac's mom said.

"Really, Mom? We're surrounded by trees!" Zac said, rolling his eyes.

"Well, you were sick of the Alphabet Game and The License Plate Game, so this one should stump you for a while." His mom laughed.

"Is it that tree?" Zac's older brother Ryan asked.

“Which tree?” his mom said, chuckling to herself.

They had been in the car for way too long, and his mom insisted they play games with her instead of playing on their devices.

Zac glanced through the rear window at the camper being towed behind the van. “How do you know I’ll be able to fit in that camper, Mom?”

“Zac, in your wheelchair, you moved around just fine, and you powered up the ramp without a problem," she said. "It's going to be fun! Stop worrying so much!"

Ryan hit Zac on the shoulder and whispered, "Lighten up. We got this! Let Mom have some fun."

Zac hit him back. His punch wasn't nearly as hard as Ryan's, but Ryan grabbed his arm like he was in pain and fell over in his seat. Zac laughed, knowing there was no way he made his athletic, football-loving brother fall, but it made him feel strong.

The camper wasn't that big, but it was better than his mom thinking she could get him in a tent. His mom was bored this summer and decided they needed some adventure. Basically, she wanted to force him outside and away from his video games. She screamed with excitement when she found an RV that was already modified for wheelchairs. She was so excited it was hard not to be happy for her, even if it meant they had to go on an "adventure."

Zac and his family arrived at the campsite, which was on top of a hill surrounded by trees. As his mom and Ryan started setting up, he drove out of the van in his power wheelchair and told his mom he was going to explore. She looked a little concerned but waved to him as he steered toward the paved trail that led down from the campsite.

The hill was steeper than Zac had first thought, but he started down anyway, ready for some excitement. As his wheelchair picked up speed, his brown hair flew in the wind. His joystick shook beneath his hand as he tried to keep control. Realizing he was about to flip forward, he leaned back in his chair, hoping his next move wasn't a somersault. Zac's seatbelt pushed against his stomach as his chair jerked to a stop at the bottom of the hill. He let out a sigh of relief. *That was a close one,* Zac thought as his heart thumped beneath his chest, reminding him of the last roller coaster he went on.

Looking around at the tall trees surrounding him, Zac continued along

the path. The hum of his power wheelchair sounded loud compared to the silence surrounding him. It was never this quiet where he lived. Back home, the houses were close together, so if you didn't hear the traffic from the road, you heard the neighbors yelling for their dog. As the birds began to sing, he realized he'd better get back before his mom started worrying. When he reached the bottom of the hill, Zac stopped. In front of him was a problem. A huge problem. The hill, with its stomach-dropping power on the way down, now towered in front of him.

How am I going to get back to the campsite? There's no way this wheelchair can power up a hill that big, he thought.

Zac pulled out his phone. No service.

He drove around to look for other campers to help him, but couldn't find anyone. The only thing he did find was himself getting lost. Zac looked around for any clue of how to get back to the campsite, but the trees that surrounded him all looked the same. Palms sweating, he thought about his next move. Looking down at the ground, he checked for tire tracks which would surely show him the way back.

On the edge of the trail, something shiny caught Zac's attention. He drove forward to get a closer look, finding a penny sitting on a rock that was as tall as his wheelchair. When he picked it up, the bushes right in front of the rock sprang open. Zac jumped up in his chair, shocked at what he was seeing. Between the bushes was a path leading to a golden well.

Is that a wishing well? Zac wondered. *There are no such things as REAL wishing wells, right?* But how did the well just appear out of nowhere? Maybe he did fall over and bump his head going down that hill! Closing his eyes, he pinched himself to make sure he wasn't dreaming.

Chapter 2

Hello Bird

When Zac opened his eyes, the well was still there. Looking around, he wondered if Ryan was playing a trick on him. Seeing no sign of his brother, Zac slowly approached it to get a better look. The bottom of the well was formed from a circle of golden stones. Green vines were growing down from the wooden roof, making it look old, yet the gold was still shiny and sparkling. Zac looked down at the penny in his hand and decided there was no harm in making a wish.

Zac thought about what he wanted. He *could* wish to be back up the hill. He *could* wish for a phone that worked right now. He *could* wish for pretty much anything. But what he knew he really wanted was an upgrade. A wheelchair upgrade. Tossing the penny in, he shouted, "I wish for the wheelchair of my dreams!"

He waited a few moments, but nothing happened. Slightly disappointed, Zac reversed his wheelchair. Just as he reached the point where the bushes had separated, his black wheelchair started glowing. Lights began shining out through his chair, and a control panel emerged in front of him with colorful buttons popping out.

"IT WORKED!" Zac shouted.

Zac's wheelchair was changing before his eyes! Excitement burst within him as his joystick slid into the arm of his chair and a new purple joystick appeared on the control panel. He reversed away from the well and his chair immediately shot backward like a rocket onto the main path. A grin spread across Zac's face. Super speed! Zooming to the left, then to the right, he raced a squirrel down the trail. *It's as fast as a cheetah—that squirrel doesn't stand a chance!*

When the scared squirrel jumped into a bush, Zac slowed down to see what else the chair could do. Which button to press next? Orange seemed like an exciting color, so he pushed it with anticipation. A robotic hand came out from the side of his wheelchair and handed him a glove. He put it on, and when he made a fist, the robotic hand made a fist too. *It looks like whatever I do with this gloved hand, the robotic hand will do too*, he thought. To test it out, he reached up and his robotic hand reached up. Zac reached higher, wondering how far it would go. When the robo-hand got to the top of the trees, Zac closed his fist with his gloved hand below. High above him, the robo-hand grabbed onto a dead branch. Zac pulled it down beside him, ducking out of the way, almost hitting himself in the face. *The cookies Mom hides on the top shelf will no longer be a problem,* he thought.

Eager to find out what the other buttons did, Zac quickly pushed the blue one. His wheels widened and grew to five feet tall. He felt like he was on top of the world! Cruising on the beach with these huge mighty wheels was going to be fun!

Zac was excited and pushed the green button next. He grabbed his armrests tight as rocket boosters shot out from the back of his chair, flying him up into the air! The wind was rushing past him so fast he thought his face would fly off! Just when his cheeks were stretching like silly putty, wings appeared from his armrests and the chair glided forward smoothly. Zac looked around and saw that a bird was flying right next to him, looking just as surprised as he felt.

"Who needs Superman when you have these mighty wheels?!" Zac shouted.

Suddenly, Zac smelled fuel, and moments later, a plane zoomed right over his head! His heart was racing. He didn't know what else lay in the clouds above, so he pushed the yellow button.

"AAAHHH!!!!" His rocket boosters stopped and disappeared back into his chair along with the wings. Zac fell straight down, the ground below him getting closer and closer, as he hoped for a trampoline to appear. Crashing through the trees, he braced for impact. His chair touched the ground, but instead of hitting hard, he bounced right back up like a bouncy ball. Looking down at the side of his wheelchair, Zac saw springs on all four sides where the mighty wheels had been.

This will be fun, Zac thought. As he bounced up and down, he saw the original hill he had rolled down. Realizing that it was no longer a problem, he pushed the blue button. The springs went back in when the mighty wheels came out. Using his purple joystick, Zac sped toward the hill. Zooming up the steep path, he quickly arrived at the campsite. When his mom and Ryan turned around to see what the noise was, their jaws dropped open at their first look at his new wheelchair.

Chapter 3

Mr. Fuzzyface

"What happened to your chair?" Zac's mom and brother shouted at the same time.

"I got an upgrade!" Zac screamed. He was about to show off his new wheels, when he heard his little dog Otto barking at a cat he spotted in a tree. Otto ran toward it, and before his mom could yell stop, Zac zoomed over, easily catching up to the dog.

Otto continued barking as Zac reached the tree, and he heard two sounds. The first sound came from the tree. "Mmmeeeeeoow." The second sound came from behind him. "Mr. Fuzzyface!" Zac turned around to see a little girl gazing up at her cat in the tree.

"Can you help me with my cat?" she asked Zac, staring at his big wheels.

Zac realized this new chair was meant to be. His wheels were already tall and wide, but they were not tall enough to reach the cat. Looking down at the control panel, he tried to remember which button would activate the robo-hand. He knew the green one was for flying, so he pressed the yellow button, hoping the glove would appear.

Instead, his big wheels changed into springs! He bounced higher and higher until he was eye level with the cat. Zac reached out to pick it up, but the cat hissed at him, so he decided to try something else before it bit him. Looking down at the control panel, Zac noticed a red STOP button, so he pushed it, hoping it would lower him back down.

His wheelchair calmly returned to the ground, changing back to its normal size. Zac breathed a sigh of relief. He looked at the little girl next to him, who now looked a bit worried.

"It will be ok, this is just a new chair for me," Zac said, trying to sound confident. "I'm sure the orange button will do the trick."

Zac slowly pushed the orange button. The robo-hand immediately

popped out of the wheelchair, handing him the glove to control it. Carefully, he extended it up the tree until it was right next to the cat. The cat refused to get on and jumped to an even higher branch, so the robo-hand had to chase it all the way to the top of the tree. With nowhere else to go, the cat jumped onto the hand, and Zac slowly lowered it down to the squealing girl beside him.

“You did it!” said the little girl, yelling thanks over her shoulder as she ran away with Mr. Fuzzyface in her arms.

After the girl left, Zac drove back to the campsite with Otto leading the way.

“What just happened?” his mom screamed, looking like she was about to faint.

“You will never believe what I found in the woods!” Zac replied, starting to describe the hill that led him to his discovery.

Chapter 4

Splash

Meanwhile, on the other side of the campground, a boy named Billy was running away from his brother, Jack. His brother was mean, always calling him names or throwing things at him. This time, Jack had just thrown a stick at Billy and hit him on the head.

His parents never seemed to care when Billy told them what Jack did, so this time he just left. His long legs

quickly took him into the woods and far from his brother. Billy was tall and running had always been his escape, not that he would tell his friends back home that. They saw him being the one in charge, coming up with funny names to call the kids with bad haircuts or who looked different from him. When he walked down the hallway at school, everyone moved to the side, no one messed with him. Too bad his classes weren't in name-calling, then his parents would actually like his grades.

After a while, he slowed down, picking up a handful of stones along the path. Aiming at a nearby tree, Billy threw them as hard as he could. A squirrel dodged out of the way just in time. Grabbing another handful, he pitched them into the bushes and heard a clinking sound. He stepped forward to investigate and saw something shiny. Pushing the bushes aside, he couldn't believe his eyes! A golden wishing well! Running toward it, he peered inside and saw some water below. When he reached in to see if there was any money inside, water splashed out, leaving Billy's shirt all wet. Could this thing be real?

There has to be money in there, he thought, so he reached back into the

well. A splash even bigger came up, and it sent him on his back. Confused and soaking wet, he got up and realized if this thing was real, why was he trying to steal a few coins when he could wish for something much bigger instead? Quickly, he ran back to his campsite. When he got there, he went in his tent and grabbed his wallet.

"What are you doing?" his brother asked, starting to get up from his sleeping bag.

"None of your business," Billy muttered and ran out before his brother could get hold of him.

As he ran back to the woods, he wondered what he should wish for. He wanted to wish for something that would make him more powerful than his brother. But when Billy reached the woods, he couldn't see the well anywhere. Where did it go? He picked up a handful of stones and started throwing them, listening for the clink again. Nothing. He picked up more stones, tossing them in every direction, his anger starting to grow. Handful after handful of stones hit trees and bushes while chipmunks darted out of the way. He continued to wildly throw them, this time spinning around to cover a bigger area.

Then he stopped.

He heard a clink!

Filled with excitement, he took off in the direction of the sound.

It appeared the bushes had doubled in size since he'd found it the first time. Squeezing his way through them, the branches scraped against his arms and legs. He pushed on until he saw it—the golden well.

Determined, he marched toward it, pulling a coin from his wallet. "I know *exactly* what I'm going to wish for."

Chapter 5

The Giant Problem

The weekend was exciting for Zac, flying around in his new wheelchair and learning what made his mom scream the loudest. His mom had been quite overprotective from the moment Zac was born, as most moms are, but especially after she found out he had muscular dystrophy. Over the past few years, Ryan had been pushing her to let Zac just be a kid. She was hesitant at first, but when she realized it was the best thing for Zac, they had been having fun ever since. His mom stopped hovering over him when he was playing with his friends and began planning family trips. If it wasn't for Ryan, Zac may never have found these new wheels.

After cleaning up the lot, Zac rushed into the van so they could drive back home. He couldn't wait to show his friend, Blake, how high he could fly!

When they got back to town, they found police cars blocking the road. His mom slowed down just as a giant boy stepped onto Main Street in front of them. Zac knew the giant from school—Billy.

"Stop the car, Mom!" Zac called from the back of the van.

"Isn't that kid in your grade, Zac?" asked Ryan.

"Yeah, he's always yelling at me and Anna to get out of his way. He thinks he's the King of the School," replied Zac.

"He looks like he's grown ten feet! How could that happen?" inquired Zac's mom.

Zac's mom parked the car and opened the back door as Zac wheeled out. He immediately saw the town welcome sign was in pieces on the road, and Billy had put a hole the size of a bulldozer into the library. On the roof of the restaurant, there was usually an enormous chicken sitting in a frying pan, but not anymore. Now the chicken was lying on its side on the roof, and the pan was in the grass, surrounded by people. Moving through the crowd, Zac saw three of his friends running toward him.

"You're way too close! You need to get out of here!" yelled Anna, who had been Zac's friend since first grade.

"What's going on? What happened to Billy?" Zac asked, ignoring her plea.

"We don't know," Cody said. Cody was shorter than most boys his age, and now looked even smaller compared to Billy. "His parents said they were camping and he came back from the woods like that."

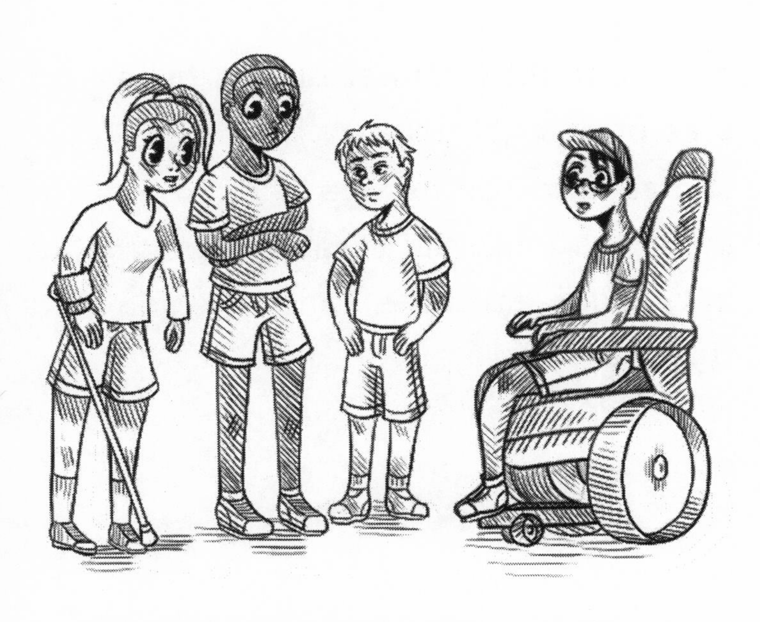

"They didn't know what to do, so they drove back to town with Billy tearing everything apart on the way," Blake added. Blake, the tallest of the four, was sweating like he had just run a marathon. "For the past hour, he's been destroying everything in his path, and the police are just holding everyone back. I've been running back and forth to my house giving my mom and auntie updates. My mom thought

I was joking with her until she saw it on the news."

Zac and his mom gave each other a curious look. Billy was camping? Had Billy discovered the same wishing well that he had?

Chapter 6

The Plan

“I have to do something,” Zac declared, and he started driving his wheelchair toward Billy.

Before he got very far, his mom stepped in front of him. “No, you do not! Just because your wheelchair is big and mighty doesn’t mean you’re ready to fight a giant!”

“Mom, you know we have to do something. I can help! I’ve been given a gift, and if I don't use it, what is the point?"

"Ok, Zac, but we need a plan. You can't just go over there without a plan," his mom said, looking around and realizing if they didn't do something, there might not be a town left for them to live in.

Zac's friends were looking back and forth at them, clearly confused. Ryan filled them in quickly as they stood there, speechless. Zac had never seen Anna speechless before, so it was a funny sight to see. She was typically waving her brown hair around while pointing her crutch at people, telling them what to do.

"So, you can fly?" Cody questioned, not looking convinced.

"You should see the birds' faces when I do!" Zac replied.

"I don't see any huge wheels. I'll believe it when I see it," Blake said.

"It's not like my mighty wheels would have fit in the van," Zac said, pushing the blue button. His friends jumped back in amazement as they watched his wheelchair transform.

"This is awesome! You could probably just roll right over Billy!" said Cody as he walked around Zac's chair, admiring it from every angle.

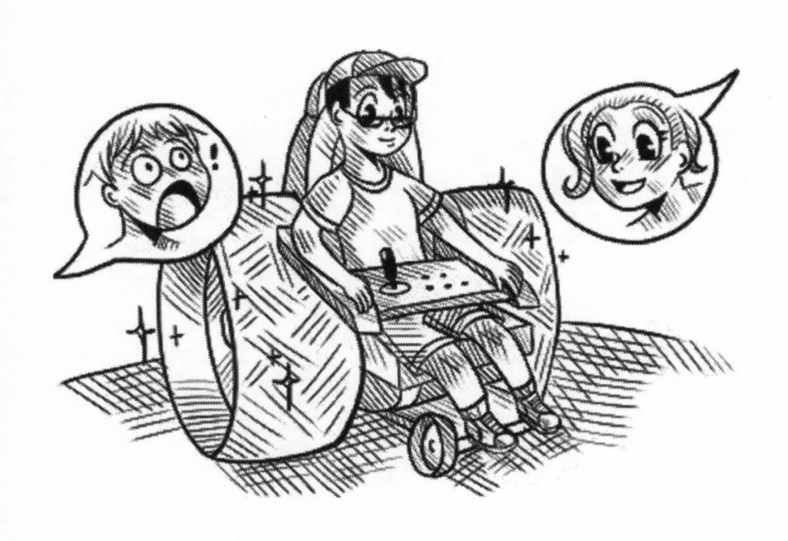

As Zac's friends admired his new ride, Ryan pointed out that Billy had turned and was heading toward the school. Looking determined, Anna quickly started coming up with a plan.

"Here's what we'll do. Zac will fly to the top of the school, cut a hole in the roof, and throw down a rope. Cody and Blake will climb up and look for Billy from above. Zac will fly through the window with me and send out his

robo-hand around the school to find Billy's location."

"That all sounds great, but he IS a giant, so we could just sneak around from the back of the school to spot him," Zac's mom said with a smug smile. That seemed simpler, so they picked her plan.

"Then what will we do?" Cody questioned.

"I wonder if Billy goes back to the well, would it shrink him down?" Blake asked.

"Wouldn't he have to *wish* to be back to normal?" Anna said. "There's no way he's doing that willingly."

"There's only one way to find out," Zac replied, gazing at Billy in the distance.

Chapter 7

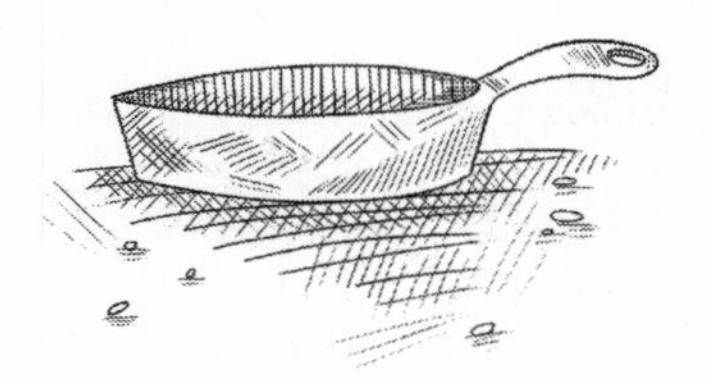

Zac Attack

Zac and his friends were closer to the school than Billy was, so they could beat him there, especially with Zac's new mighty wheels. Pushing the purple joystick forward, Zac sped ahead of his friends with Anna hitching a ride on the back of his wheelchair since she couldn't run as fast. Anna wanted to scream, but she put her head down and closed her eyes, driving past the

police, who were setting up barricades to slow Billy down. Zac was going way too fast, in Anna's opinion, but she didn't want people spotting them and ruining their plan.

Zac went around to the back of the school but realized he had to confront Billy, and the only way to do that was face to face. After Anna got off the wheelchair to wait for the others, Zac sped to the front of the school.

The barricades were no match for

Billy, tossing them out of the way as he strolled toward the school. Panic filled Zac as Billy loomed over him, looking huge and monstrous.

"What do you think you're going to do, Zac?" Billy laughed.

"I hear you found a wishing well," Zac said. "Not sure if you heard, but I found one too."

A look of curiosity filled Billy's eyes. "You don't look any different, besides those big wheels. Why should I believe you? Besides, that well was really hard to find—the bushes would have been too tall for you to even see it."

"The bushes sprang open for me to find it. Are you saying you had to search for it?" Zac questioned.

"Of course I had to search for it! Not just anyone can use a wishing well. You have to earn it!" Billy yelled, getting more frustrated.

Zac was starting to understand what happened. The wishing well wanted him to find it, but Billy's discovery was just an accident. "Billy, the bushes grew taller so you couldn't find it. You got lucky. For me, the bushes sprang open. I think I'm supposed to have these powers."

"Doesn't look like it, little boy. All you're doing is sitting there," said Billy as he looked down at Zac.

"What are you doing with your powers?" Zac shouted back. "Looks like you're just trying to destroy things, like usual! It's time to go back to the well and fix this."

"No way, I'm not going back to the well. I'm going to destroy this school!" Billy ran to the building and smashed the corner of the roof with a powerful punch. As the pieces flew in the air, Zac saw his friends and family come around the corner with their arms over their faces, blocking the rubble.

Zac quickly drove over to meet them. "We have to get him back to the well," he said. "If we can knock him down, I can fly him back."

"We are going to knock that beast down?" Blake questioned, his typical confident manner changing into a look of fear.

"We are," Zac replied, looking around and seeing the giant frying pan from the restaurant. Classic. "And I know how we're going to do it! Cody, Mom, and Blake, run and get that frying pan. Anna and Ryan, find a rope from the gym."

They ran off in opposite directions and Zac drove toward Billy. "You don't have to do this. We can help you, and you can use your powers for good!"

"Get out of here, Zac!" Billy yelled and took a swing at Zac to move him out of the way. Zac reversed backward, easily moving out of arm's reach. Billy looked surprised, but quickly recovered and pulled his arm back to aim a punch at Zac.

In the distance, Zac saw his friends struggling with the huge frying pan. He pushed the green button on his

control panel and flew above Billy. Billy, although shocked at seeing Zac above him, thought Zac was flying to get away, so he turned his attention back to the building.

Zac flew to his friends, using the purple joystick to move easily around the trees. At the campground, he had learned that after shooting up into the air with the rocket boosters, he could push his joystick forward and it would pop the wings out immediately. No more silly putty face. Pushing the orange button, he grabbed the glove as it shot out. Quickly putting it on, he extended his robo-arm and grabbed the enormous pan. He flew back to Billy, staying far enough away that Billy didn't see him coming. Throwing wasn't his thing—that was Cody's skill—but he lined up and threw it right at Billy.

"Sunnyside up!" Zac yelled.

Billy was about to take another punch at the school and didn't see the pan coming. Bam! The enormous frying pan struck him right on the side of his head. He fell to the ground, knocked out. Anna and Ryan ran out with the rope and started tying him up.

"Egg-cellent hit, Zac!" Cody yelled.

Once Billy was tied up, Zac and his friends rolled him into the frying pan for transport back to the well.

"You sure you can do this, Zac?" His mom looked worried when she realized she couldn't go with him.

"You know I can," Zac said confidently.

"You're right. Leave now before he wakes up!" Zac's mom said, as Ryan gave him a pat on the shoulder.

Chapter 8

Take Back

Flying while carrying a giant was not easy. It took all the rocket booster power Zac had, so the flight was bumpy. Holding the pan with his strong robo-hand, he moved the joystick to avoid each building. When more trees appeared below, he knew he was getting closer. Thankfully, Billy didn't wake up until the campground was in view.

"AAAHHHH! Let me down! Let me down!" Billy screamed.

"What? Never flown before?" Zac asked as he flew up high and did a wobbly loop while Billy continued screaming. Zac realized he may not have enough rocket power for that, so he slowed down to balance them out.

Spotting a familiar spot in the woods, Zac pushed the red button. Landing gracefully, he dropped the pan. Keeping Billy tied up, he drove over to find the well, and immediately, the bushes sprang open once again to reveal the golden well. The well was more beautiful than he remembered, glistening in the sunshine. This time, though, Zac could feel it was not for him. It was tempting to ask for more than he already had, but he could sense that the well opened up for Billy.

"Why are we here?" Billy asked.

"Billy, you know the well wasn't for you. It gave you powers, but you used them to destroy our town. Why?"

Billy paused. "I felt powerful. It was fun scaring my brother for once. You should have seen how fast he ran away when he saw me for the first time!"

"Why do you want to scare your brother?" Zac asked.

"Oh, you know, for things he's done to me. Like pushing me into a pool, throwing sticks at me, chasing me down to push my head in the snow, stuff like that." Billy shrugged.

Zac felt a twinge of regret for the loopty loops he did as they flew above the well.

"I get that. But even without your new powers, you had a way of scaring everyone at school."

"Yeah, so what? Better to be the one picking on people than to be picked on yourself." Billy's anger was starting to boil again.

"But is it worth it? Are you happy being a bully like your brother?"

"Well, most people are afraid to talk to me anyway. I think even my best friends might be scared of me." Billy was quiet for a minute. "So, I guess this giant body won't help in that way. Fine, Zac, what do we need to do?"

"I'm new at this too. I assume you make a wish to go back to your old self?" Zac smirked at Billy and added, "Or maybe nicer than your old self?"

Billy laughed and Zac started untying him. The ropes dropped when Billy got up from the frying pan. His huge shoulders slumped as he slowly started walking toward the well. He didn't look very confident, and Zac wondered if he would do the right thing.

When he got to the well, Billy turned around to Zac. "Aren't you forgetting something?"

"Oh yeah!" Zac reached in his pocket for a quarter and extended it to Billy with his robo-arm.

Billy turned to the well, took a deep breath, and threw the quarter in. Zac heard him mutter a wish, but couldn't make out what he said. Billy closed his eyes, feeling his arms starting to shrink back to size. He peeked through one eye and saw his hand getting smaller. The grass was moving closer as his legs shortened, and he was no longer able to see the tops of the trees. Zac looked at him with relief.

Billy turned to Zac, "Let's go home."

Chapter 9

Even Superheroes Have Rules

That night, Zac sat down for dinner with his family. They were talking about his ride back to town with the normal-sized Billy and how they started cleaning up Main Street together. There was still a lot to be done, but it was a good first step.

"Do you think you will become friends with Billy now?" Zac's mom asked.

"I don't know. He has a lot of changing to do, which he said he wants, so I would be willing to try." Zac paused before adding, "He did wish to go back to normal without me forcing him to."

"Remember, Blake and Cody didn't make good decisions when you first met them either. They sure used to give their teachers a hard time."

"Oh, yeah. They started a lot of fights back then, but they came around when they realized being nice brought them more friends and more fun."

"You must be a good influence on people." His mom looked deep into his eyes. "But this superhero stuff is something entirely different. You need to be careful."

"What's your idea of careful?" Zac asked with a grin.

"I want you to have at least two friends with you at all times. They will help you make smart decisions. I don't want you dealing with bad guys, but if you can help people, then you need your friends with you."

That seemed like something he could agree to. At least she didn't say he wasn't allowed to fly.

"So now what? Let's go to a big city with some real danger! I need to get busy being a superhero!" Zac said.

"Not a chance!" his mom said. "This city seems to be enough excitement for all of us."

Laughing, Ryan joked, "Maybe a family of giants will come!"

"Or maybe an alien will beam down from space, or maybe all the grandmas will disappear!" Zac exclaimed.

His mom and Ryan rolled their eyes at Zac for his wild imagination. It was fun to joke around, knowing this was a quiet town and a giant was the first excitement it had ever had. The real question was, would it be the last?

About the Authors

Andrea Kurth is a special education teacher from Michigan who realized her students weren't often represented in books and wanted to change that. Inspired by her students, she set out to create a fun series where the story is the focus, not the disability, and is filled with adventure for younger children but exciting enough for the older struggling reader. When Andrea isn't teaching or writing, she enjoys traveling with her wonderful husband and sons. Visit her at www.kurthbooks.com for free lesson plans.

Owen Kurth is a creative seventh grader. He could play the guitar, piano, and violin if he learned how to play the guitar, piano, and violin. So instead he enjoys playing video games with friends and spending time with family. He aspires to be a movie writer and director one day.

About the Illustrator

Emily Gudzinski is from South Lyon, MI and studying illustration at Kendall College of Art and Design. After finishing her degree, she plans to continue creating mixed media using a variety of mediums. By designing artwork that challenge uncovered topics in society, Emily will use her art to create meaningful pieces that will show appreciation in things she is passionate about. Visit her at www.instagram.com/makochaitea

About the Editor

Nadara "Nay" Merrill is a Texas resident who spends her days editing, drinking coffee, and reading. She also enjoys walking her dogs, Ranger and Copper, and snuggling with her cats, Cosmo and Saturn. Growing up, Nadara's favorite subject in school was English, which is where she discovered her love for the written word. After earning her bachelor's degree in English, she started a freelance editing business in order to help authors reach their writing goals by ensuring that their books are in the best shape as possible and ready for publishing. Her services include line editing, copy editing, and proofreading for children's books and full-length books. Visit her website at www.thatgrammargal.com for more information.

Made in the USA
Middletown, DE
29 May 2021

40625195R00043